Alice

ISBN: 979 864 264 679 3
Imprint: Independently published
©2020 by Ilia Tskhvediani

Publishing : Quill (Internet publishing)

E-mail : intpub20@gmail.com

Short description

Alice a girl from a big city from Germany. Travels to the big city of New York City planning to explore and expand her horizons. But little did she know that there was a pandemic making its way around the world. And that she would be stuck in a country far from home and the ones she loved. She struggles and sees how a virus can take away people's humanity and turn the world a cold place.

Alice

Alice, a humble and wanderer girl from the city of Frankfurt known for their modernistic skyline finds her way into another city famous for their skyline New York City, she went there as a graduation present from her parents who wanted her to explore the world and to expand her horizons.

She arrives at the JFK airport where no one is waiting for her, she wanders and follows the direction that a friend of her mother gave her and found the right line to go from the JFK to Brooklyn where she would be spending the next month and a half.

Everything was fine for the first couple of months, she was able to go to the museums in the first weeks and stores that were well known back there. She wandered through the enormous streets of new york city, getting lost in the crowd of Times square and amazed by the wonders and everything she found on her way.

One morning her parents woke her in the middle of the night, talking about a situation where a virus was spreading from a country in Asia that was making its way to European countries, it had already hit Italy and Spain and was making its way to Germany, her parents sounded scared but she remained calm. She explained how the city was more alive than ever, how there were many tourists walking on the streets, and there was no news or report about the alleged virus.

Her parents serenaded by her words, as she was the one connected to the internet and was a smart girl, they wished her no harm and to let them know if she needed anything or heard something about the virus. She told her parents to take care as well and she would hit them up if something changed.

The next couple of days everything remained normal, people walking around and going to the market, Alice kept going to her exchange classes about international business, she had found it at the time of her arrival and there were vacancies so she joined before the group closed.

There were other foreigners in the group, at first she remembered there were over 20 participants but now the numbers had lessened and they were probably just 10 students. There was an Asian student who was really nice with everyone and always participated, but the last couple of days he had been sitting away from the group and some of the other participants were telling him to leave or go away.

Alice was startled about this but didn't worry too much about it, it seemed that people still acted racist for no particular reason, that's why she had maintained a low profile during the course and just spoke when it was needed. Avoiding any unwanted attention.

She was staying in an Airbnb apartment that had several rooms just for girls. The owner was an old lady named Rebecca. She was really nice with all the girls and made breakfast for all them every morning.

After the situation in the workshop she noticed that there were fewer girls in the Airbnb, and the remaining ones weren't even leaving their rooms. What was going on, that she was so ignorant? That same night she received a text from her mother, letting her know that the virus had spread into their city, there were a couple of people sick, but not dead yet. Alice decided to look into the information and found out how many people were dying all around the world because of this virus.

Was this the reason people had stopped to show up on the workshop and the same reason her roommates weren't leaving their rooms. She looked online and read that the virus was transmitted by droplets from sick people, surfaces, the air, or any contact with an infected person. The precautions were to wear a mask, gloves and wash hands constantly. She hadn't been doing any of that, she wasn't feeling sick. But people were locking themselves avoiding physical contact, why was the country not on lockdown, there wasn't any news or protocol by the President.

Alice decided to take her own precautions even if there was no protocol, if she kept herself safe, she could do her regular activities. She went out to buy groceries the next morning and found a tremendous line outside, so she decided to skip that market and walk to the one that was two blocks away. When she got there, there was an even longer line outside. Some people were wearing masks, but others weren't. She waited in line and after an hour she was able to walk inside.

People were taking toilet paper with them, it felt like an apocalypse, everything was empty. She was able to get some canned food, bread, and water with her. Someone sneezed close to her and she saw the panic on everyone's face. They walked away from that person and that's when she started to feel panic.

She paid and walked as soon as she could back to her Airbnb, she left her groceries on the floor and avoided touching her face or anything with her hands. She walked straight to the shower, where she took a long shower and washed every inch of her body. Once she got out she organized her belongings in the little fridge in her room.

A phone call startled her, from her mother. She doubted picking up, she didn't want any bad news. But if she didn't her mother was going to worry without a reason.

— Alice?, her mother sounded scared.

— What happened?

— This virus is spreading too fast Alice, people are dying within days, the hospitals are full of people. Please come back home.

Alice still had three more weeks left in this country, and her workshop wasn't over until 2 more weeks.

— Mutter I can't, the workshop we pay for isn't over until 2 weeks, As soon as it's over I'll go back home.

— Alice..., take care.

— Danke Mutter.

Alice hung the phone and laid on her bed, she looked at what she had bought, that wasn't going to be enough for the remaining weeks, she would need to return to the supermarket, she didn't have masks, she had brought some gloves for the cold weather which she hadn't used. She looked for them and placed them on her nightstand. She looked on her belongings, some thick clothing she could wear. And made a list of everything she needed.

Masks, gloves, hand sanitizer, more food.

She looked for more information online and the virus was spreading, the numbers in the USA had been increasing in the last week, shit was getting serious.

The next day at breakfast, Alice walked out and saw Rebecca, their hostess cleaning the table.

— "Where is everyone, Rebecca?"

— "Some of the girls are trying to return home, a group tried to go to the supermarket now that it is early and 2 of them are locked in their room."

— "Do you think this is serious?" Alice asked her.

— "I have never seen anything like this, people are acting crazy as if it's the end of the world, essentials are gone by the minute the markets open, it's getting harder to buy things and the lines are endless in the supermarket. I have never done a line in my life to go to the supermarket" Rebecca admitted as she sat on the table.

— "Are you feeling OK?" Alice asked her, she kept her distance and she was afraid Rebbeca might be sick.

— "Oh yes, I'm just thinking that I'm running out of my meds and need to go to the supermarket, but everything is so packed that I don't even know what to do."

Alice could tell Rebbeca was really worried about the situation, maybe not about getting infected but how hard it was going to be for her. An old lady does things she used to do in the morning, could take her a whole day while also putting herself at risk. She was among the vulnerable population.

— "I could help you if you need help." She decided promptly, she was healthy and she could help her, she had been too nice with all of them.

— "Thanks, you don't need to." Rebecca stood up from the table and Alice could see the wrinkles in her face and skin. She wasn't as young as Alice had thought, she could be in her 60's.

— "But, I want to, just tell me what you need and I can go and get it for you. I also need to buy some things, I need hand sanitizer and masks."

— "Oh, I have both, I could lend you some as a way of thanking you for helping me with that."

Alice smiled at her and waited for Rebecca to go to her room and gather a surgical mask with a small bottle of hand sanitizer. Rebecca wrote down a list of the things she needed and where she could go to gather her meds, as Alice drank a warm cup of coffee.

Rebecca handed her everything. Alice made sure her gloves had no holes and that the mask was tight enough, she left with a backpack she had brought with her and walked out, heading to the unknown and madness of people who were afraid about a virus that was living among them.

Alice walked through the now less crowded streets of New York City, the city seemed like a ghost town, walking next to supermarkets and pharmacies it did look like an apocalypse was happening. She kept her distance from everyone, and kept her hands in her pockets. Making sure she didn't touch any surface or anyone on her way.

The place she had to go to get the medicine of Rebbeca wasn't far from there, there was a line outside. She waited, some people were not respecting the distance, they were literally next to each other, these people, if they didn't keep their distance they could get sick and not show any symptoms until it was too late.

Breathing was almost impossible with the mask covering her mouse and nose. But she didn't take it off, she tried to take slow breaths to calm herself and get air. She played some music through her headphones, she was going to need to wash them as soon as she got back. But made sure to not touch anything else.

It was her turn, she handed the prescription and the woman asked her for Rebbeca, she told her she was staying at her place, but Rebecca wasn't with her, the pharmacist told her she needed to be with her to pick up her medicine.

— "But I have the prescription, she is an older woman she wasn't going to come here and put herself at risk and everyone living in her apartment."

— "I understand Miss, but she needs to be present so we can hand you her meds."

Alice took a deep breath, she hadn't come all this way to leave empty-handed.

— "Listen, I know you are following a procedure, but is there a manager or someone I could speak to," She had made her mind this lady wasn;t going to help her. She rolled her eyes before walking to the back room and dragging a young man probably in his 30's, wearing a robe, a mask, and gloves. In fact they all were wearing that in the pharmacy.

— "How can I help you, miss?"

— "Hi, I came here to gather meds from my grandmother, she needs her medicine and I told her to stay at home as you know this virus affects more older people, she is in her 60's. I brought her prescription and she even gave me her medicare card."

Alice handed everything to the manager and stared at him waiting for an answer as he looked at all the documents.

— "Thanks, let me see what I can do."

Alice felt relief washing over her body, she had made it. She waited for the pharmacist to hand her the medicine and take her money. She walked out of the pharmacy and felt dizzy all of a sudden. She stood still and rested on the wall next to the pharmacy, trying to breathe and calm herself. People were watching her weird, she didn't want people to think she was sick or something.

The supermarket she was heading to wasn't far away, another long line. But this one took less time than previous ones, she was in and out before she noticed. The place was a mess, people almost fighting for goods, again no toilet paper left. She didn't understand why people were taking that, she was able to get a box of gloves and more hand sanitizer she was going to need that and more, but there weren't many left and she thought of those who came here and needed it more than her, so she just took one box and one bottle.

On the line to pay she saw the cashier had gloves on, she touched money, passed groceries, and used the machine. The gloves were dirty, Alice could swear it even had a hole in it. But she decided not to look at them too much, otherwise, she wouldn't be able to go through with it.

She picked some goods for her on the way and walked back. There was a commotion near her Airbnb, she tried to slow down and find out what was going on when she noticed there was a body lying on the floor. People were recording but no one was helping, the person seemed to be out of air.

— "Someone call 911."

Alice heard a woman screaming out, some were keeping their distance, others covering their faces, but not all had masks or gloves, they were exposing themselves to this. But this person didn't deserve this treatment, she tried calling 911 but her phone didn't have service.

— "Someone call 911" Alice screamed, a young adult next to her took out his phone and called. She stood within the distance from him, making sure this man got the right help, it was difficult no one dared to get close to him. Alice heard him explain.

— "There is a man lying on the street, gasping for air. No one had approached him, everyone is afraid he may have the virus."

Alice stared at him and gave him a nod. She looked around, some people had walked off leaving this poor man alone. This virus was going to turn people into less warm humans. People walked away from him, not even looking at the body. It seemed unreal, as if a deadly virus one from those movies had become real and now people were turning into zombies as their hearts were now cold and only cared for themself and no one else.

Alice saw the ambulance arriving and some paramedics wearing full gear bring this man into the ambulance, but he was being treated as a terminal patient. They were too afraid he had the virus which was a big possibility.

The hall was empty as she entered her Airbnb. It was all quiet, it felt empty but she knew she wasn't. Maybe everyone was in their rooms avoiding physical contact. She walked to the kitchen where she found Rebbeca drinking some tea, she saw how her face light up as she saw Alice, she walked to thank her.

— "Wait, it's better you wait for me to take a shower, I was out there, you could wash with alcohol or disinfectant everything I brought, in case someone infected touched them."

— "Yes, you are right."

Alice could see how her expression switched from happiness to concern. But they all needed to be safe and that was the only way she could think of keeping anything away from them. That she had worn gloves and masks didn't mean that everything she touched hadn't been touched by someone infected.

She ran to the shower and ripped all her clothes and left them on the corner, she would need to clean all that later.

Alice rubbed her skin until she was 100% sure she was clean and off any bacteria. Her skin hurt as she scrubbed harder and harder. But she kept replaying the scene of that man lying on the floor defenseless, no one helping him. And how everyone looked at her outside the pharmacy. She couldn't get sick, she needed to follow every protocol to keep herself safe. She was supposed to go to her workshop that afternoon, just the idea of walking out there exposing herself and then returning home to this again stressed her. But she needed to.

Rebbeca was accommodating everything she had brought her, Alice placed in the common fridge her goods.

— "Thank you so much for this, I don't know how to thank you for it, did they give you trouble at the pharmacy?"

— "You bet they did, I had to talk with the manager, I told him there was no way you were going out there to risk yourself and he gave me everything without questioning."

Alice felt great with herself, she knew her mutter will be proud of her, she imagined her parents out there alone, who would help them, she needed to help the ones who didn't have no one, she might not be able to help everyone. But helping Rebecca was a way to start as well as it was making them call an emergency for that sir.

Alice prepped herself again, now on a pair of jeans, boots, her gloves, mask, and a brown sweater and walked out. She was afraid of taking the subway as it was a common space and it was more auspicious to contamination and or spreading the disease, all those bodies together, holding the bar, sneezing, touching everything. Just thinking about it gave her a headache.

It took her almost 40 minutes to get to the place where her workshop was given. But it was worth it, it was open and she walked in to find it completely empty. Less than 5 students had attended, the facilitator greeted her as she walked in. Everyone was sitting with 2 chairs apart.

— "Thanks for joining Alice, as I was telling this would be our last class, we would have to continue with an online platform, we don't know when yet, but we won't be able to continue from here as the situation isn't very favorable and the attendance has lessened within the last week to almost a 20% percent."

Alice was disappointed, but she kinda saw it coming if people were locking themselves at home, weren't schools and jobs supposed to do it as well. The lesson of the day was short, she didn't want to write anything down, nor on her phone or notepad. She paid attention and was going to write a summary once she arrived back in her room.

— "Thanks for coming, please check your emails. You should be receiving a notification with further instructions, sorry for everything on the name of the institution and be safe."

The facilitator started to gather her belongings, she saw some of the guys chatter keeping their distance but still thought was it safe? Alice walked out, took a picture of the email in case she might need it for later, on her way out.

Streets were empty, just a couple of people were walking around the time square, mostly tourists that were taking advantage of the empty streets to get their photos. If you looked at it in that way. It has its perks, the streets were emptier therefore there was less garbage and less pollution from native and tourists.

She stopped and took a picture of the empty time square, it looked as many of those movies she had seen back home where an illness attacks the US and everyone is dead or in lockdown. But the only difference was that this time it was real, it wasn't fiction or part of a movie. It was really happening.

Alice avoided crossing paths with people, she kept aside walking near the street or the empty crosswalk. There were still lines at supermarkets and fast food restaurants. Some places were closed like cinemas, while some clothing stores were open but with very little customers.

The world was changing, this wasn't the same city she had arrived in, a few weeks ago. This was a whole different place, people were changing or had to change the way of behaving. She could see those who kept their distance and tried to avoid physical contact with others. We had to put aside our affection and turn into an apathetic version of us. One that didn't greet people, that stayed away from others and avoided any contact with other human beings.

All this crossed Alice's mind as she walked humming a soothing song, and trying not to see desperate people in lines who seemed to be waiting forever and those who came with barely nothing on their hands, probably because they didn't find what they were looking for or because they couldn't afford anything else.

Once she arrived home, she heard a TV on and she approached it, where she heard the news. Establishments that promoted social interaction will be closed until further notice, malls, gyms, movie theaters and similar will be shut down. As well as companies that weren't necessary.

It wasn't a mere illness or a conspiracy theory this was getting real and the governors had noticed and now started to state demanding protocols. Which were going to create concern and fear among the citizens and everyone in this country now. Airports were shut down to, until the end of the month for now. No incoming or leaving flights were allowed.

Alice was thinking about leaving on the next plane to Germany which wasn't a possibility at the moment. Her return flight was scheduled in two weeks but now she was condemned to stay here for 2 more weeks or more. This was not something she had planned, it was 10 PM in Frankfurt, but she decided to text her parents.

Airports are closed until further notice, they say they will reopen at the end of the month. But I'm not sure, have airports closed there as well?

She waited for a response from her mother, but she didn't reply. Alice didn't want to think the worst but in this situation that was all she could think of. She called, but there was no response from their end. None when she tried calling her father.

She went and took a shower, making sure she felt clean enough. Her skin seemed to be developing some type of rash from the constant scrubbing and cleaning. But she prefered an ugly rash rather than getting sick.

The next couple of days Alice decided to stay indoors, she wanted to make sure she didn't have the virus and at the news said it took two weeks for it to incubate and for the first symptoms to show up, she decided to avoid any physical contact with other people and go outside.

The news and social media were full of information, fake news and recommendations towards the virus. It felt too much and Alice felt overwhelmed. She decided to watch a movie, something that kept her mind off it for the next couple of hours.

Next thing she remembered was her phone vibrating next to her, she had fallen asleep watching the movie and it was now 4:50 am which meant it was 10:50 over there, she had 5 missed calls from her mother and tons of messages.

Are you OK?

Alice?

Where are you?

Please tell me you are safe!

ALICE YOUR DAD AND I ARE WORRIED.

ARE YOU SICK?

WHAT'S HAPPENING ALICE, PLEASE ANSWER.

Her texts were like that, her hands were shaking and she had a horrible headache, she walked to the bathroom, washed her face and drank a glass of water before sitting on bed and writing her mom back, she wasn't in the mood to talk. She felt a weird sensation on her throat.

— I'm fine, sorry I fell asleep. I'm in my room. I put myself on self quarantine for the next two weeks, to make sure I'm not sick or develop any symptoms. Are you and papa taking precautions?

— Yes, Alice we are. We had to go to the market and it was full of people, I think there are sick people out there. I'm scared, please be safe. Write to me when you can.

— I will mutter, take care. Please, don't go out if it is not necessary.

Her mother didn't reply anymore. Alice went back to bed where she spent her whole day. She didn' get out of her room for the last 3 days. Waking up, taking showers to keep herself fresh, drinking water and energetic drinks. While looking for entertainment, tv shows, movies or silly games that kept her main distracted.

It wasn't that hard at first, standing up from the bed, trying to do a 5 minutes workout routine to keep her body active, go take a shower, eat something, go back to bed, watch a tv show or a movie or play something. Then stay until late, sleep and then wake up the next day to do everything again. She was able to keep this routine for the next 3 days, but then she started to feel trapped. Needing air and to go outside. But she was scared of getting sick as the numbers of sick people rose up and more and more people were dying everyday from the virus.

She walked to the living room on the 4th day and found Rebbeca sitting there by herself. She seemed worried and alone. How many people were out there all by themselves, with no one to talk to, losing their mind slowly. That's how Alice had felt in her room the past three days and now walking out and seeing Rebbeca all by herself made her wonder if that was the right choice.

— "Are you OK?" Alice asked as she took a seat facing Rebecca on the table.

— "Yes, a couple of friends and relatives are positive with the virus, one of them is in an intensive care unit." Alice could tell how her voice broke when she said those words, probably she hadn't spoken to anyone in the last 2 days.

— "I'm sorry to hear that, I can't imagine how hard it is for you."

— "Yeah and her husband can't even go to the hospital, he has to stay home and wait to hear from the hospital till she recovers or worse." Rebbeca started sobbing and Alice felt her heart break a little, how sad was all this.

Not being able to be with your loved one as they remained unconscious on a bed, not knowing if they were going to get better or die. And what happened after they died was worse, their family couldn't see him and maybe not even have a chance to say goodbye to their loved ones.

This virus wasn't condescending, it was rough, it was mean. It had no space for kindness.

Alice tried to walk out of her room to spend some time with Rebecca who felt alone, the other girls were staying in their rooms. One of them hadn't left in a whole week. People were isolating for the best, but Alice was scared it was going to affect people in a psychological way.

They were running out of goods, within a week of her last visit to the supermarket. She didn't know what the other girls were eating or drinking. She knocked on some of their doors and they just told her to go away. Alice got worried thinking if they were sick and that's why they didn't want to have contact with anyone or they were just trying to avoid getting sick.

At this point it was hard to tell why people were isolating, because they had contracted the disease or afraid of getting it.

She made a list of everything she needed to get, this time she tied her gloves and mask, making sure nothing was loose and giving no space for this virus to enter her body. She had a light breakfast, took her bag and walked out.

As soon as she walked out, she felt as if she had traveled in time. The streets were empty, silent and clean. She could hear the birds singing and other animals walking around. Nature had regained its space, the air felt different, cleaner.

Alice walked around the now ghosttown of New york city, not a soul on sight, she saw people gathering around food markets and it felt like a zombie apocalypse. People craving for food and essentials, everything else wasn't important. It felt unreal, she wanted to be home with her parents. Not stuck in a town that didn't speak her language, nor felt like home.

Arriving at the supermarket, felt like chaos. There was a line but people were all over the place, still she saw people unprotected, shopping as if everything was OK. When it wasn't.

The line took forever, she heard people speaking about magical cures, drinking garlic, making gargles with warm water, drinking chloroquine pills, and some other recommendations that they were receiving through social media. She tried to not pay attention to what they were saying. It was unbelievable how gullible people could be during a pandemic.

Alice walked in the store, it was emptier than last time she came, they weren't letting everyone come in. It was a total of 20 people tops per turn, and once a group of 5 left they let more people in. At least they were controlling the flow of people, because some didn't respect the Social distancing.

She walked through the supermarket halls, trying to find some necessary supplies, but some were harder to find than others, she had to settle for low fat milk, instead of whole milk because there wasn;t anymore. Dairy products were almost gone, there was no cheese, and the bread left seemed too old.

She thought of what could replace the things she was looking for, and bought things that could help her to survive another week and a half, and some of the things that Rebecca had listed for her.

She looked around, some people wearing homemade masks, wearing ripped shirts, boxers, bags, headbands, anything to cover their mouth and nose. But she wasn;t sure about the effectiveness of those. Were they safe enough to protect them, she didn't know and was afraid to find out they weren't.

That night after she arrived, she helped Rebecca disinfect everything she bought and organized it and took some of her stuff to her room. She made herself a bowl of oatmeal with some fruit banana and kiwi and brought it to her room, she decided to turn the news. And everything was about the virus.

The hospitals were over capacity, there were thousands of casualties just in one week. THe numbers were elevating like a roller coaster. And now The USA was higher in numbers than European and Asian countries where the virus originated.

She was worried about her parents, the numbers in germany were high, but were under control the last couple of days, her mother sent her a contact about an airline taking people back home, she contacted them and they told her at the moment there wasn't any plane designed home.

Her airline had cancelled her ticket and told her she could request for a full refund, but there weren't any flights going to her destination in the next couple of days, and they didn't know when flights to Germany were going to be available. United States had closed borders with European and Asian countries. She didn't know until when she was stuck here.

She didn't have much cash left on her, but she was afraid of going to a bank in this situation. That's when one morning she approached Rebbeca who was sitting on her balcony.

— "Good morning, Rebbeca, How are you feeling?"

— "Bad, my friend passed away, last night. Her family is devastated, they can't see her. They won't be able to say their farewells."

Alice wanted to comfort her, but was afraid of the physical touch.

— "I'm very sorry, that must be horrible for her family and loved ones."

She heard Rebecca sobbing and snoring on a handkerchief, it felt wrong not being able to see someone who passed away, not knowing where their body was going to rest. Not having a proper burial ceremony.

— "You don't need to worry about paying for the extra time here, I know you can't travel home yet."

She heard Rebecca saying, she didn't know how to thank her for it.

— "Thanks, Rebecca, I can pay you for the extra days,"

— "Don't be silly child, you have helped me enough, I'm the one who can't repay you for risking yourself for this old lady."

Alice wanted to hug Rebecca but she sent her a mental hug instead.

— "How are your parents?"

— "Worried, my mother sent me some information, hoping I can catch a humanitarian flight back home as commercial flights are cancelled until further notice."

— "Yes, I have some friends stuck in the caribbean, even an old neighbor who went on a cruise, had to stay there for over 2 weeks, with sick people and even dead, No country had wanted to allow them disembark."

— "That is terrible."

— "Yes, I don't know what's happening with humanity, we are forgetting that we are dealing with human beings and keeping the sick away like this doesn't mean we remain safe, what about those who are healthy, they will get sick or worse in those conditions."

— "That's true, we are turning into an appatic version of us, we are not caring for others, just for ourselves."

— "That's exactly how it is."

That night, she avoided the news. But people still posted the numbers on their social media, everyone was a news reporter now, updating everyone about what was going on in the world. How many dead people, how many sick and how many recovered. The numbers in NYC were higher than other cities, people were dropping dead everywhere.

There wasn't a cure, the only recommendation was to stay home, proper cleaning and avoid touching our faces while outside. It felt like a bad dream, Alice wanted to wake up from. But this was a reality, as cruel as anything, anyone could have ever imagined. It feels right from a horror movie or novel.

Alice was keeping herself safe, two weeks after and no symptoms. She made sure Rebecca didn't leave the apartment and she helped her with everything she could, some of the girls had been able to return home. Others were still in their rooms, walking out every couple of days for some human connection while keeping their distance.

Alice's parents texted her everyday, asked her how she was doing and she asked for every detail and how they were keeping themselves safe. She made sure they followed every procedure from wearing gloves and masks, to throwing them away once they arrived home, leaving their shoes at the front door and throwing all clothes to the washing machine as soon as they arrived home. She wasn't home but that was the closest thing she could do to keep her parents safe.

In the last week of April, she woke up to a text from her embassy, there were forming groups and sending people back home. She was going to be put through several tests to make sure she wasn't ill before boarding and once she arrived home, she had to go through forceful quarantine and then get tested within 2 weeks of her arrival, to make sure she wasn't to expose people back home.

She agreed to the terms, she packed her stuff, told goodbye to Rebbeca and called a taxi to the airport. It wasn't the safest way to get there, but she wasn't going to walk, nor she pretended to take the subway.

On her way to the airport, she looked at the empty city, which was famous for being awake, everyday, now was sleeping, people on their homes, stores and restaurants closed down. Many without a job, while others spend their solitude time alone, craving for human contact, while they couldn't. Many people have died and many more will die as well.

She just wanted to be back home, together with her family, before she came here, she was excited about traveling abroad, being away from her bored hometown and her noisy parents. BUt now all she could think of was getting back to the warmth of her house, the hot cocoa from her mother in the morning and listening to her father listening to his old tv shows.

She prayed for those who were alone, who couldn't see their family and for those who were stuck in another country like her. That the universe or any God heard their callings and gave them strength to go through this situation and that soon they returned to their families.